SCIENCE AND SORCERY

A DESTINY DO-OVER DIARY

EVER AFTER
Royals!

THIS BOOK
BELONGS TO

_____

EVER AFTER
Rebels

SCIENCE AND SORCERY

A DESTINY DO-OVER DIARY

Suzanne Selfors

LB

LITTLE, BROWN AND COMPANY

New York   Boston

Little, Brown and Company

Hachette Book Group
1290 Avenue of the Americas, New York, NY 10104
Visit us at lb-kids.com

Little, Brown and Company is a division of Hachette Book Group, Inc.
The Little, Brown name and logo are trademarks of Hachette Book Group, Inc.

The publisher is not responsible for websites (or their content)
that are not owned by the publisher.

First Edition: April 2015

Library of Congress Control Number: 2014955129

ISBN 978-0-316-40133-3

10 9 8 7 6 5 4 3 2 1

RRD-C

Printed in the United States of America

EVER AFTER
Royals!

Professor
Rumpelstiltskin

EVER AFTER
Rebels

Dear students,

I am your teacher for Science and Sorcery! I teach you how to make potions!

I don't like students! I don't like teaching! I like gold! I like to have lots and lots of gold! I give pop quizzes, and if you fail, you go to attic and weave straw into gold for me!

If you complain about me to Headmaster Grimm, I make you weave more straw into gold!

Rules that must be followed in my classroom:

- Don't ask questions! They give me headache!
- If I take nap, don't bother me!
- If you make big explosion or sticky mess, you clean! I don't like to clean!
- If you wear gold, I take! I like gold!

If you break rules, I send you to attic to weave straw into gold!

Good-bye!

Professor
Rumpelstiltskin

WARNING FROM
HEADMASTER GRIMM
Students of Science and Sorcery:
Please be advised that you should
NEVER promise your firstborn child
to Professor Rumpelstiltskin.

A GINGER WELCOME

HI, EVERYONE!

Ginger here.

I'm so glad to meet you. I can tell already that you're a creative person, just like me. This journal will give you lots of ways to express yourself. Don't be afraid to try new things. Go off book every once in a while. Just because a recipe calls for something doesn't mean you can't still add your own ingredients, your own spices and flavors. This is a good lesson in life, I think. How else are you going to figure out what interests you?

Remember, even if your mom is a Candy Witch like mine, you don't have to follow in her bootsteps. Whether you've found a secret recipe or you're simply doing it the old-fashioned way, with determination and hard work, you can choose your own destiny.

HAVE FUN.

Ginger Breadhouse

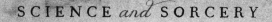

DEAR DIARY
GINGER

Ginger has a huge crush on Hopper Croakington II, but she hasn't found the courage to tell him how she feels. Even though he works the camera during her *Spells Kitchen* MirrorCast, she still feels shy around him.

Can you pretend that you're Ginger and imagine a day when you've told Hopper how you feel? How did you do it? What was his reaction?

Dear Diary,

GINGER'S GOWN

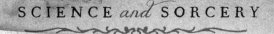

Ginger is creating a gown for the Thronecoming dance at Ever After High. Ginger likes to dress the same way she decorates—with bright colors, icing swirls, and candy buttons. What do you think her dress would look like? Using markers and colored pencils, create a gown for Ginger. Don't forget to add accessories, such as jewelry and a hat.

WITCH SWITCH #1

Ginger's mother, the Candy Witch, looks
like most wicked witches, with green hair,
a ragged black dress, and a hairy wart on
her chin. But when Ginger was a little
girl, she desperately wanted her mother to
look like other mothers.

Imagine that you brewed a potion in
Science and Sorcery class that would
allow someone to have an instant
makeover. What would the new Candy
Witch look like?

MAGICAL TOUCH

The world of Ever After High is a combination of real technology and magic. Students communicate with cell phones (MirrorPhones) and use tablets (MirrorPads), just like we do. Some students walk to class, but others fly with their fairy wings.

In the book *Kiss and Spell*, Ginger mixes ingredients by hand but cooks them over a dragon flame. And although she studies traditional subjects such as Evilnomics and Crownculus, she also learns how to make magical recipes in her Science and Sorcery class.

If you could add a few fairytale touches to your school, what would you do?

SCHOOL LOCATION	FAIRYTALE TOUCH
school cafeteria	
football field	
teachers' lounge	
locker	
library	
your favorite school club	

Now give your locker some fairytale touches.

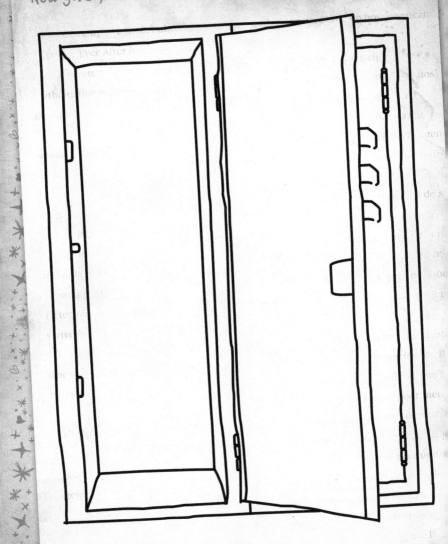

Decorate a locker for a friend, too.

BAKE SALE

The members of the Ever After High Tech Club didn't make any money with their kissing booth, so they've decided to try a bake sale. Ginger offered to make some delicious cupcakes, but—uh-oh—her mother got to the bake sale first and left some rather unsavory-looking treats.

Take these ordinary cupcakes and turn them into something that might have come from the Candy Witch's kitchen.

BLONDIE LOCKES WORD SEARCH

Look for these words in the puzzle—can you find them all? Words may appear up, down, across, backward, or diagonally!

PORRIDGE

JUST RIGHT

TOO HOT

TOO COLD

SNOOPING

JUICY SECRETS

GOLDEN CURLS

THREE BEARS

REPORTER

GOLDILOCKS

```
S T E R C E S Y C I U J S R
G O L D E N C U R L S R Q T
O T P O R R I D G E A K R L
L R H B S Q D X M E L T T J
D E W G R N N R B L T Y N M
I T R Y I P O E T O H O O T
L R M D G R E O O D W W D J
O O M K R R T C P D Q R B B
C P R W H K O S N I L M G W
K E M T P L Y D U J N K P R
S R Q M D L R T M J D G M L
```

DEAR DIARY
♡ MS. BREADHOUSE ♡

Ms. Breadhouse is visiting a nearby village with her daughter, Ginger. She's trying to fit in, but it's not easy—she's actually the infamous Candy Witch. Instead of shopping for glass slippers or going out to lunch, she'd rather spend her days concocting poisonous recipes.

Imagine that you are Ms. Breadhouse and your day went terribly wrong. You tried not to draw attention to yourself or embarrass Ginger, but something happened and now the villagers are scared of you.

Dear Diary,

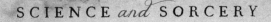

TAKE THE TIME

Ginger has a saying at the end of her MirrorCast:
Life is a piece of cake if you take the time to bake.

Ginger's telling us that it's important to take time for the special things in life. But we live in a world where everyone seems so busy and so many things distract us. If you could bake a wish cake and make a wish to have just a little more time, what is the one thing you would focus on? How would that change your life?

SPICE YOUR LIFE

Have you ever heard the saying that variety is the spice of life?

Herbs and spices come from all over the world and are used to add flavor to food. They can transform an ordinary bowl of noodles into something sweet, hot, or tangy. Cinnamon and nutmeg give us the flavors of winter. Vanilla bean and mint remind us of spring.

If you were a spice, which would you be and why?

Can you make up some magical spices that Ginger might use in her recipes?

You Only Live
Once Upon A Time

SPELLS KITCHEN

Humphrey Dumpty fell off his chair. He's okay—it's only a small crack—but you must take his place as the director of *Spells Kitchen*. Unfortunately, viewership has plummeted because everyone is watching Daring Charming's reality show, *Daring's Day*.

As the new director, you need to attract viewers. What are you going to do?

Here are some ideas:

- Bring in a special guest.
- Choose a recipe for Ginger that is hexciting or dangerous.

Once you have your plan in place, write the episode!

SPELLS KITCHEN
Episode 14

Director: Cue theme music.
Lights! Camera! Action!

Ginger: Welcome to *Spells Kitchen*.
I'm Ginger Breadhouse, and on
today's show I'm going to...

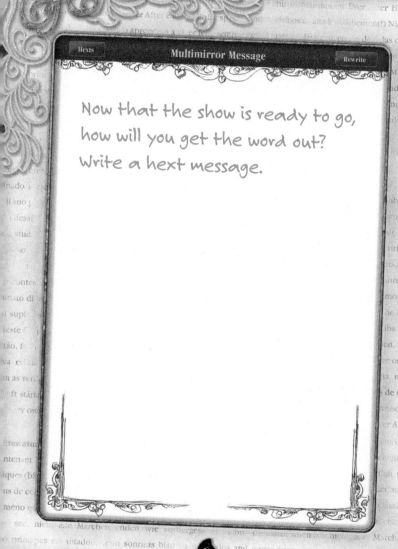

Multimirror Message

Hexts   Rewrite

Now that the show is ready to go,
how will you get the word out?
Write a hext message.

PICK YOUR PASSION

Ginger is a great example of someone who has made time in her life to do something she loves.

You don't need a magical recipe from Science and Sorcery class to be like Ginger. Each of us has the same potential. You might already know exactly what you love to do and can imagine yourself taking that passion and making it a central part of your life.

But maybe you're not so sure. Perhaps you need more time to figure out what your passion is.

Why not start thinking about it now? Make a list of things that you're good at, or things that make you happy. Cut out this list and put it on your wall next to your bed or above your desk.

Things I Love to Do:

Things I Love to Do:

Things I Love to Do:

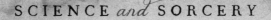

WITCH SWITCH #2

When the Candy Witch visits the beauty parlor, the hairdresser is shocked to find all sorts of things in her hair—tangles, twigs, and a toad! Yuck!

Draw other objects or critters that might be hiding in her hair.

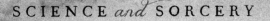

BE THE STAR
OF YOUR SHOW!

If you were a student at Ever After High and were given the opportunity to host your own MirrorCast, what would it be? Do you have a talent you'd like to share with other students? Would your show be serious or funny?

Title of your show:

Now write your first episode:

Director: Cue theme music.
Lights! Camera! Action!

You:

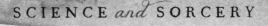
SPIN A SOUND TRACK

Melody Piper is Ginger's
roommate. She listens
to music everywhere she
goes. In a way, she's always
creating a sound track
of her life. If you could
create a sound track for the
following events, which
songs would you choose?

1. Theme song for Ginger's MirrorCast cooking show, *Spells Kitchen:*

2. A song for when Hopper is crushing on Briar Beauty:

3. Theme song for Daring's MirrorCast show, *Daring's Day:*

4. A song for when Ginger is crushing on Hopper:

5. A weird or scary song for the Candy Witch's entrance:

SOUND TRACK OF YOUR LIFE

Now that you've created a sound track for the characters of *Kiss and Spell*, what songs would you choose for a movie about your life? List the moment and the song you'd choose.

Maybe it's a song for when you're hanging out with your best friends forever after. Or maybe it's one for when you're talking to the boy or girl you like.

MOMENT	SONG

HUMPHREY DUMPTY WORD SEARCH

Look for these words in the puzzle—can you find them all? Words may appear up, down, across, backward, or diagonally!

EGGHEAD

FRAGILE PRINCE

TECH CLUB

RAPPER

BREAK HIS CROWN

HARD-BOILED

DUMP-T STUDIOS

KING'S HORSES

SCRAMBLED

OFF BALANCE

```
F R A G I L E P R I N C E B
D U M P T S T U D I O S R T
S E S R O H S G N I K E M O
D D M T W R N B D D A R F B
E L E Q E D A A Y K B F N T
L X R L R C E P H R B Z R Z
B R T T I H H I P A N G M K
M Y L X G O S C L E W Y L N
A T N G Y C B A L Y R L Y M
R Y E M R T N D P U Q W N W
C X G O Q C Q T R Y B D D Q
S Y W D E P Q Z T A R B Q J
N N B Y N J Q Q P N H Z D D
```

JELLY JARS

Ginger has a very strange pet named Jelly.
Jelly is a candy fish that, thanks to a magic
spell, believes he's a real fish. While he
doesn't breathe oxygen or eat fish food,
Jelly does like to swim.

Can you create a fun world for Jelly?
Turn these jelly jars into mini fish tanks.
Maybe one has a castle. Maybe one has a
plastic shark. You decide.

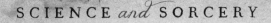

DEAR DIARY
✳ HOPPER ✳

Hopper is a prince, but he often doesn't feel like one. His unfortunate curse is that he changes into a frog at the most embarrassing moments—when he tries to talk to girls.

Have you ever found it difficult to talk to someone you liked? Did you get nervous? Did the wrong words come out? If so, then you can probably understand how Hopper feels each time he tries to talk to Briar.

Imagine that you're Hopper and you've just had *the* most embarrassing encounter with Briar. What happened?

Dear Diary,

SPELL-CIAL DELIVERY

About once a week,
Ginger goes to the
mail room at Ever
After High to pick
up a special delivery.
She orders ingredients
for her cooking show
from places all over
the fairytale world. If
you were Ginger and
could order something
hextra-special, what
would it be?

TO:
GINGER BREADHOUSE
EVER AFTER HIGH

CANDY MOUNTAIN CHOCOLATE

CANDY MOUNTAIN CHOCOLATE

CANDY MOUNTAIN CHOCOLATE

TO:

TO:

TO:

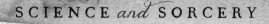

REBEL RECIPES

The students at Ever After High often find themselves divided between those who are Royals and those who are Rebels.

What does it mean to be a rebel? Rebels aspire to flip their scripts and rewrite their destinies. Sometimes, moving in a direction that is different can yield a positive result.

Would you label yourself a rebel? Can you remember a time when you stood up for something you believed in or you went in a direction that was different from the one your friends chose?

Write about it here.

REWRITE, IGNITE

Hopper gets embarrassed pretty easily, and when he blushes, he turns into a frog.

Most of us have had an embarrassing moment (or two or three) that we'd like to forget. But what if there was a recipe in Professor Rumpelstiltskin's Science and Sorcery class that allowed you to go back in time and redo that embarrassing moment?

Here's your chance to rewrite the moment you'd love to do over.

RE
Write

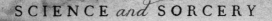

♥ HEART 🖤 CUPCAKES ♥

It's Lizzie Hearts's birthday, and Ginger is making special cupcakes for the occasion. Here's a simple way for you to make heart-shaped cupcakes, lovely enough to serve to a princess of Wonderland.

What you need:

- Cake batter (made from a box cake mix, any flavor)
- Cupcake liners
- Cupcake pan
- Glass marbles
- Frosting (any flavor)
- Sprinkles (optional)

What you do:

- Mix the cake batter according to the package's directions.

- Place liners in the pan. Fill each one until it is half-full of cake batter. Do not overfill.

- Place a marble between the pan and the lining paper. This creates an indentation in the baked cupcakes that is the top of the heart shape.

- Bake according to the package directions.
- Let the cupcakes cool, then frost and decorate.

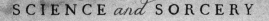

OH CURSES!

Hopper is a royal prince, but his curse is that he changes into a frog whenever he blushes.

Is there a creature you'd like to turn into? Write a scene in which you become that creature for the first time.

Is there a creature you'd hate to turn into? Write a scene in which you become *that* creature for the first time.

SCIENCE *and* SORCERY

You Only Live
Once Upon A Time

POTION PRACTICE

In Ever After High's Science and Sorcery class, students spend a lot of time learning how to follow recipes that include magic potions.

If you were in Professor Rumpelstiltskin's class, what magic potions would you want to concoct?

Create potions that some of the students might like to use.

Hopper's Potion

Directions: Add a thimbleful of this potion to soup or stew, and it will give you the ability to talk to girls without blushing!

Hopper's Potion

Directions:

Rumpelstiltskin's Potion

Directions:

Blondie's Potion

Directions:

Melody's Potion

Now create a
potion for yourself.

Directions:

Invent more potions here:

Directions:

Directions:

TONGUE TWISTERS

When he's in frog form, Hopper has no trouble talking to girls. In fact, he's quite poetic. But when he's in human form, he can barely get the words out. His tongue becomes tangled, and he ends up totally embarrassed.

Do you ever feel as if your tongue is tangled? Here are a few tongue twisters. Can you say each of them ten times fast?

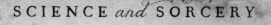

Forever is forever ever after.

Freshly fried flying frog.

Potion perfection.

Bad blood, good blood.

95

Can you make up a few tongue twisters?

You Only Live
Once Upon A Time

SCIENCE AND SORCERY POP QUIZ #1

Professor Rumpelstiltskin is in a grumpy mood, as usual, and he's giving the class a pop quiz. If you get 100 percent of the answers correct, you won't have to spin straw into gold. But if you are incorrect on one or more answers, then you'll be stuck in his attic spinning straw all day! Good luck.

DRAW A LINE TO COMPLETE
EACH SENTENCE.

1. A spell is

2. Sorcery is

3. A potion is

4. Gold is

5. Students are

6. The Candy Witch is

a. the art of
   conjuring magic!

b. annoying and not
   likable!

c. the best thing in
   the world!

d. the liquid form of
   magic!

e. the best cook in
   the world!

f. the verbal form of
   magic!

Answers: 1. f, 2. a, 3. d, 4. c, 5. b, 6. e

DEAR DIARY
❀ BLONDIE ❀

Blondie is very proud of her MirrorCast, *Just Right*. It's the show to watch for the latest Ever After High gossip. She spends a great deal of her time snooping around, trying to uncover secrets. She always wants to be the first to get the scoop!

Can you imagine that you are Blondie and you've just learned that Ginger has a crush on Hopper? This is big news! No one has ever admitted to having a crush on the frog prince. You know that revealing this will bring in a lot of viewers for your show. But it will also hurt Ginger's feelings. What should you do? Write about this dilemma.

Dear Diary,

POISONOUS PICNIC

The Candy Witch is an expert in the kitchen, and she loves creating wicked recipes.

In *Kiss and Spell*, the Candy Witch agreed to go on a date with Professor Rumpelstiltskin. She packed a special picnic—imagine some of the horrid things she brought! Let's look in her pantry. Can you create some new ingredients?

Bog water

Pickled worms

SCIENCE *and* SORCERY

Now it's time to create some wicked recipes that Professor Rumpelstiltskin is sure to like.

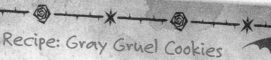

Recipe: Gray Gruel Cookies

Ingredients:

- 8 cups oatmeal
- 3 handfuls sludge
- half a bucket swamp water

RE Write

Directions: Mix together and cook for two weeks in a cauldron. Do not stir!

The lumpier the better.

Side effect: Turns the eater gray.

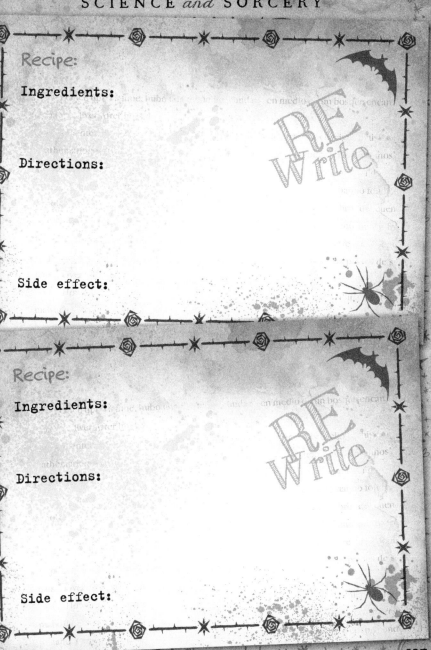

Recipe:

Ingredients:

Directions:

Side effect:

Recipe:

Ingredients:

Directions:

Side effect:

Now that all the cooking is done, it's time to go on the picnic. Create a horrid picnic worthy of the Candy Witch.

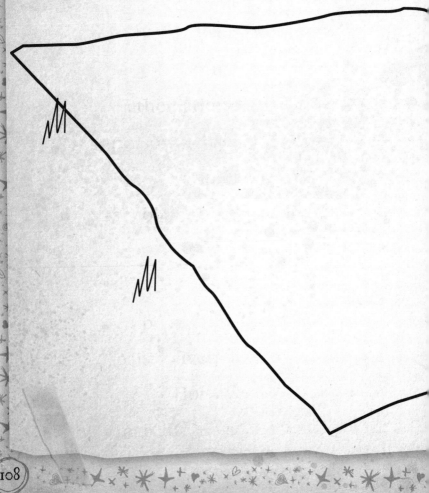

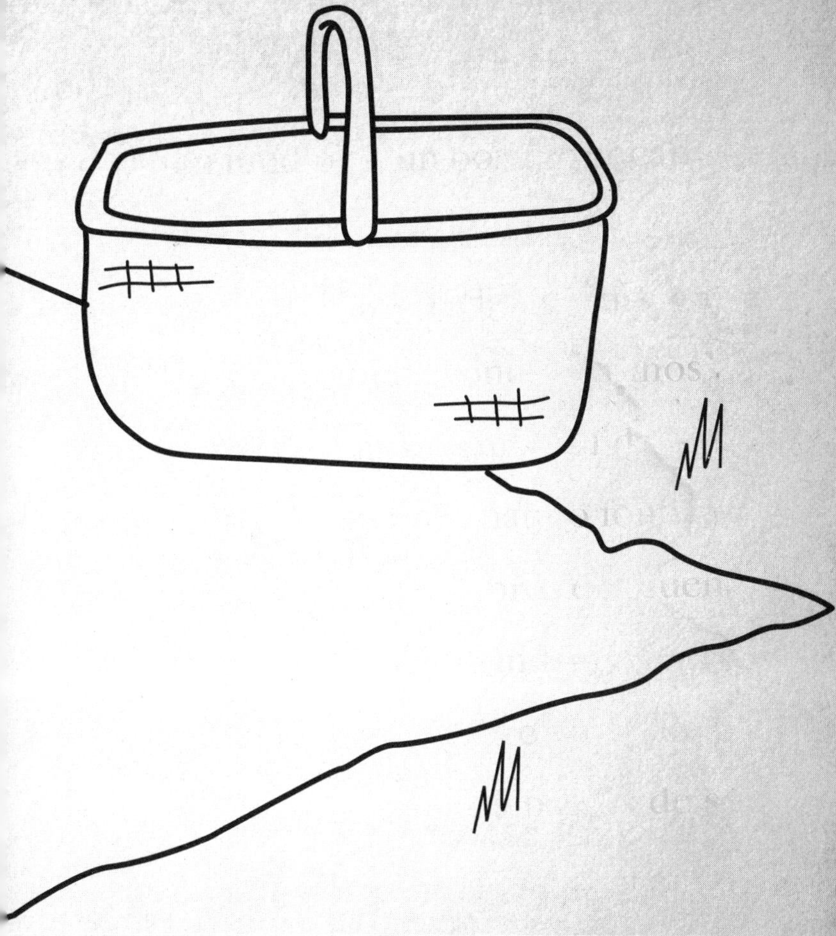

BEST FRIENDS FOREVER AFTER?

Ginger and Blondie are good friends, brought together by their common desire to have a successful MirrorCast. They get along great, but sometimes Blondie has trouble keeping secrets.

Actually, Blondie *always* has trouble keeping secrets! She wants to reveal everything on her MirrorCast, *Just Right*. Ginger understands that Blondie wants to have a good show, but it hurts Ginger's feelings when Blondie can't keep any of Ginger's secrets.

Have you ever told a friend that his or her secret was safe with you, but then you spilled it? Would you like to rewrite that moment?

EVER AFTER
Rebels

Imagine that you've found a special recipe in Professor Rumpelstiltskin's Science and Sorcery class — it allows secrets to be taken back. Write a scene in which you use this recipe and your friend's secret remains safe.

REBELS

GINGER'S NEW LOOK

While hosting her MirrorCast show, *Spells Kitchen*, Ginger wears an apron to protect her clothes from getting stained and covered by things like fairyberry juice and singing sprinkles.

Design some cute aprons for Ginger. Remember that she loves lots of decorations and color.

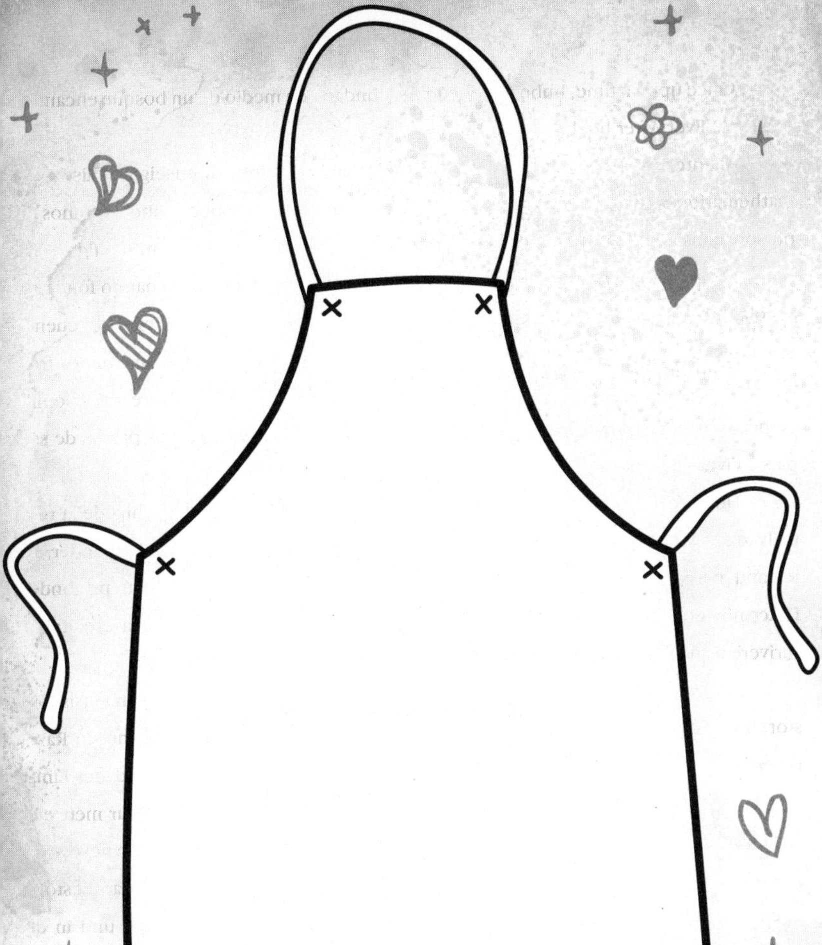

SCIENCE AND SORCERY POP QUIZ #2

Professor Rumpelstiltskin is in an even grumpier mood than usual because he threw all his clothes into the dragon-breath dryer and they shrank! So now his britches are too tight, his hat is too small, and his shirtsleeves reach only to his elbows.

He's giving another pop quiz. If you fail, you'll get stuck sewing new clothes *and* spinning straw into gold.

DRAW A LINE TO COMPLETE EACH SENTENCE.

1. I get angry vhen

2. I get extra-angry vhen

3. I get super-duper angry vhen

4. I get so angry that steam comes out of my ears vhen

5. Do not bother checking answers, because

a. my boots are too tight!

b. I have no gold!

c. I miss episode of *Housewives of Troll County*!

d. I skip breakfast!

e. you all fail!

HOPPER WORD SEARCH

Look for these words in the puzzle—can you find them all? Words may appear up, down, across, backward, or diagonally!

SLIMY

KISS

POET

CURSE

FLY BREATH

PICKUP LINES

LONG JUMP

BLUSH

PRINCE

SWAMP

DRAGONFLY

B L C U R S E B N T M D K
L Q X P T K Q T K N V Q X
T J Q L M Y L J W V S P D
H P M U J G N O L E R R B
L T J B Y J T P N Q A Y L
S Z A L P B J I P G M K B
P W V E G V L G O I R R L
R L A G R P X N L P N B N
I D M M U B F S H T W V V
N L L K P L Y S N K E K Z
C X C N Y N U L R T I O L
E I L N N L R Y F S Z X P
P J Z Z B Q Z X S D G Y B

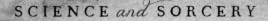

CINNAMON TROLLS

One of Ginger's favorite treats to bake is a batch of cinnamon trolls. These Ever After High versions of gingerbread men are easy and fun to make.

What you need:

- 1 roll sugar cookie dough
- Cinnamon sugar
- Vanilla icing
- Food coloring
- Icing bag and nozzles for piping the icing (optional)
- Candies of your choice (optional)

What you do:

- Using a floured rolling pin, roll out the sugar cookie dough onto a lightly floured surface.

- With a gingerbread man cookie cutter, cut out your cookies and place them on a non-greased cookie sheet.

- Sprinkle each cookie lightly with cinnamon sugar.

- Bake according to the directions on the dough package.

- Now turn your cookies into trolls! Divide the icing into batches and tint with food coloring. Use green for the troll's face, hands, and feet.

- Choose whatever colors you'd like to decorate the rest of the troll. Remember that trolls have big noses, bad teeth, and hairy chins (both boys and girls).

  If you wish, decorate with small candies.

SCIENCE *and* SORCERY

Here's an example of what a girl troll and a boy troll look like. You can copy these or make up your own looks. It's up to you!

KISS ME #1

In *Kiss and Spell*, Hopper wishes to be turned into a frog forever after, and his wish comes true. But according to his story, he can be changed back into a prince by the power of a single kiss.

Kisses are an important part of fairytales. Sometimes the kiss must come from a prince or a princess, and sometimes it must be a true love's kiss. Can you match these famous fairytales to their equally famous kisses?

DRAW A LINE TO COMPLETE EACH SENTENCE.

Famous Fairytale Kisses

1. A girl sleeping in a glass coffin is kissed by

2. A girl asleep in a tower is kissed by

3. An amphibian is kissed by

4. A mermaid who wants to be a human girl wants to be kissed by

5. A grumpy old man named Rumpelstiltskin is kissed by

a. a prince who fell in love with her singing voice.

b. a prince who searched the forest for her.

c. no one! He's gross!

d. a princess.

e. a prince who fought his way through a thorn forest to find her.

Answers: 1. b, 2. e, 3. d, 4. a, 5. c

KISS ME #2

Why are so many problems in fairytales solved by a single kiss? Obviously, that doesn't work in the real world.

Rewrite the ending to a famous fairytale so that it's not a kiss that solves the problem, but something else.

Sleeping Beauty

Remember, she's fast asleep and locked
in a tower. When the prince arrives,
he wakes her with a kiss. How would you
rewrite this story?

REBELS

You Only Live
Once Upon A Time

DESTINY DO-OVER

Whether a hero or a villain, a Royal or a Rebel, each student at Ever After High asks the same questions: What do I want to do with my life? Do I want to follow the path that others have paved for me, or do I want to find my own way to a Happily Ever After?

Create a destiny do-over for each
of these students:

Ginger Breadhouse

Ginger is destined to become the next Candy Witch,
but Ginger really loves to bake and share her spellicious
treats with all the students at Ever After High.

What kind of destiny can you reimagine for her?

EVER AFTER
Royals!

You Only Live
Once Upon A Time

Hopper Croakington II

Hopper is a royal prince who is destined to turn into a frog and then be kissed by a princess, thus living Happily Ever After and ruling his kingdom.

That sounds like a great story, but Hopper wants more control over his destiny. He wants to be able to talk to girls and, therefore, find his own love, not someone who just happens to come along and kiss him. What kind of destiny can you reimagine for him?

RE
Write

Blondie Lockes

Blondie seems to have her act together. She's doing what she loves—starring in her own MirrorCast, *Just Right*. But Blondie doesn't have a big fairytale ending to her story. No Happily Ever After has been carved out for her.

If Blondie could rewrite her destiny, she'd give herself a Royal Happily Ever After.

What kind of destiny can you reimagine for her?

Now create a destiny for yourself.

You don't need to be a student in Science and Sorcery to ignite your destiny. While we don't live in a magical world, we make choices each and every day that influence our futures. It's time for you to imagine a destiny for yourself. The magic belongs to you!

SCIENCE and SORCERY

EVER AFTER
Royals!

$\mathcal{D}$on't miss the novel that goes
with this hextbook!

Read **Kiss and Spell** by Suzanne Selfors
to find out what destiny awaits
Ginger Breadhouse and
Hopper Croakington II!

CHOOSE YOUR OWN EVER AFTER

Discover the World of Ever After High™

WATCH ON NETFLIX

Ginger Breadhouse™
DAUGHTER OF THE CANDY WITCH

Blondie Lockes™
DAUGHTER OF GOLDILOCKS

Check your local retailer for enchanting dolls and products!

 EVERAFTERHIGH.COM
Play games, watch videos and meet the spellbinding students.

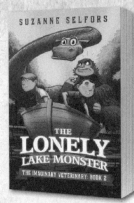

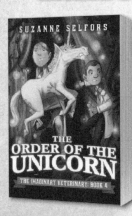